The Wonderful World of Disney

Walt Disney

LADY
AND THE TRAMP

DERRYDALE BOOKS
New York

Twin Books

Many, many years ago, on a snowy Christmas morning, Jim Dear and Darling celebrated their first Christmas together. They had just been married, and had no children yet.

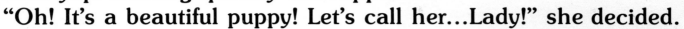

Jim Dear handed Darling a huge present, out of which came a little yap. Darling quickly unwrapped it.
   "Oh! It's a beautiful puppy! Let's call her...Lady!" she decided.

Darling and Jim Dear were very happy with Lady, and Lady with them. She spent the winter inside the house, but when spring came, she was allowed outside. One morning, she met her neighbors, Jock the Scottish terrier, and Trusty, an old bloodhound. They were purebred dogs too, and they had a lot to talk about.

But then one day, Lady found a scruffy looking dog in her backyard.

"Hi, Pigeon! I'm Tramp," he said, and then, seeing Lady's puzzled frown, he quickly added, "I'm not a purebred dog...

...and I don't wear a collar! I'm free as can be...

...and I sleep where I please! Every day is a party, Pidge! Why don't you come with me? We'll have fun together!"

Lady sent Tramp on his way with a firm no. "Thank you, but I'm very happy where I am," she told him. And how right she had been to refuse him, because a few months later, Darling gave birth to a beautiful baby.

"Lady! Come say hello to your new friend!" called Jim Dear, beaming with pride. Lady ran up to the crib. She was very careful not to wake the baby when she took a peek.

"What a beautiful baby," she thought. "We'll have lots of fun playing together when he grows up!"

The weeks went by and Lady was very happy.
"You're such a good dog," said Darling one morning, patting Lady on the head.

"Now don't be too sad tomorrow when Jim Dear and I leave on vacation. We'll be back very soon, and Aunt Sarah will be here to look after you and the baby. So be good and look after the house!"

Lady did not understand what Darling had told her, but she wagged her tail to show Darling that she was happy.

The following day, Jim Dear and Darling packed their bags. Lady was not happy that they had gone without her, but then she thought, "They left me behind to take care of the baby and the house. I'll make them proud of me!"

But then Aunt Sarah arrived with her two Siamese cats, who were not a bit friendly.

The two Siamese cats were wicked. As soon as Aunt Sarah left the living room, they started to scratch the furniture, tear the curtains apart, and knock over everything in their way. Lady was shocked. She growled furiously when they tried to knock the canary out of his cage. When they tried to fish the goldfish out of his fishbowl, she started to bark, hoping Aunt Sarah would come back.

Her barking did not stop the cats, but it did alarm Aunt Sarah.

She came running into the room, and the Siamese cats immediately sat still.

"Oh, my goodness! What happened?" she cried. The Siamese cats meowed and pointed at Lady.

"You bad dog! How dare you attack my darling cats! I won't let you hurt them. You'll be punished for this!" shouted Aunt Sarah, furious. Lady was heartbroken, but the Siamese cats were very pleased with themselves.

The following morning, Aunt Sarah brought Lady to a pet store. She held her down while the shop owner fitted her with a muzzle.

"Wonderful! Now she'll leave my cats alone!" said Aunt Sarah. Lady was terrified. She struggled wildly while Aunt Sarah tried to hold her still.

Lady had been treated kindly all her life, and she couldn't understand why these people were being so cruel. She began to struggle with even greater strength. She pulled at her leash until Aunt Sarah had to let go. The old lady screamed, but Lady was already far down the street, running as fast as she could.

But all of a sudden, a pack of stray dogs, seeing that she was defenseless, cornered her behind a barrel. They were ready to attack.

But before they could hurt her, Tramp appeared. "You cowards!" he growled. "Pick on someone your own size!"

The dogs slunk away, ashamed.

"I've got a friend who'll take that muzzle off in a cinch!" said Tramp, and he led Lady to see the beaver at the zoo.

"Yeah, chewing is my job! You'll be free in a second," promised the beaver as he dug his sharp teeth into the leather. The muzzle soon snapped loose and Lady was free.

"Thank you so much," she said. Then turning to Tramp, she added, "Thank you too, Tramp! You saved my life."

"Don't mention it, Pidge! It was my pleasure," replied Tramp. "Why don't we go and celebrate at my friend Tony's restaurant?"

Lady gladly followed Tramp down the street. She was beginning to like him a lot.

Tony owned an Italian restaurant. He served them a delicious spaghetti dinner by candlelight and played romantic songs while they ate. Lady was dazzled.

After their meal, Tramp took Lady for a walk under the stars.

"This has been a wonderful evening," said Lady. "Thank you for helping me out."

"You don't need to thank me. I've enjoyed myself, too," said Tramp. "But why are you here with me and not with your family at home?"

"It's a long story," began Lady, and she explained to him what had happened to her since Jim Dear and Darling left.

"That's awful!" said Tramp when she was done. "I'll make sure nothing like that ever happens to you again!"

They slept under the moon and the
stars, and watched the sun rise at dawn.
"I think I should go home," said Lady.
"Maybe Jim Dear and Darling are back."
"But not before we've had breakfast!"
said Tramp mischievously. "I know where
we can get fabulous fresh eggs!"

"This is it!" said Tramp standing in front of a hen house. He started to dig under the fence.

"But it doesn't belong to us!" protested Lady as Tramp slipped into the hen house. The hens started to cluck loudly.

Tramp barked, laughing, and the hens flew about in a panic.
The racket brought the farmer over.

"Tramp, the farmer! Quick!" cried Lady. Tramp jumped out of
the hen house and ran away, but Lady was not so fast.

The farmer caught her and called the
dog pound. They took Lady away.

Lady was desolate. She felt that Tramp had betrayed her, and the dog pound was an awful place. The other inmates tried to cheer her up by singing a funny song but Lady was not amused.

"Don't worry, Babe!" said one of the dogs. "With a collar like yours, you'll be out of here in no time!"

Just as the dog had said, Lady was taken home the following morning. Aunt Sarah had called the dog pound and because Lady's name was engraved on her collar, they had been able to identify her.

"Good-bye and good luck!" said the dogs.

Lady was touched, but very pleased to be leaving. She was anxious to go home and find out if Jim Dear and Darling had come back.

But when she arrived, only Aunt Sarah and her wicked Siamese cats welcomed her. "You wicked dog! I won't allow you back in the house, and since you don't want to wear a muzzle, I'll tie you up to the dog house!" said Aunt Sarah, furious.

Lady was utterly miserable. "Even Tramp let me down!" she thought sadly. She lay in the doghouse until night fell. Then, all of a sudden, she saw a large rat crawl to the house.

The rat jumped into the baby's
bedroom through the window. She ran
after him, barking wildly, but her chain
stopped her short, choking her.

"What will happen now?" she thought
in a panic. "The rat will hurt the baby!"
She barked as loudly as she could.

Just then, Tramp showed up. "Help!" cried
Lady. "A rat went into the baby's room!"

Tramp jumped into the baby's room after the rat, growling and barking. The rat attacked him, but Tramp managed to strike back. By the time Lady broke free from her chain and came into the room, the rat was dead. Tramp gingerly licked his wounds.

Just then, Aunt Sarah burst into the room, holding a broom in her hand. When she saw Tramp and Lady, she screamed.

"What did you do to the baby, you wicked dogs? I'll get you for this!" she cried. "This is terrible! What will Jim Dear and Darling say?"

She pushed Tramp into the closet with her broom and locked Lady in the basement. Then she called the dog pound.

The dog pound wagon came and took
Tramp away immediately. Lady could
hear Tramp's desperate and angry barks.
She did not know what to do and started
to cry. But then she heard familiar voices
in the hallway. Jim Dear and Darling
were back!

They let Lady out and she quickly led them to the dead rat in the baby's room. "These dogs saved our baby's life!" cried Darling. Aunt Sarah was confused and apologetic. Jim Dear called a cab and set out with Lady to the dog pound.

Poor Tramp could not believe that he
had lost his freedom. But all of a sudden
two dogs attacked the carriage.

Jock, the Scottish terrier, and Trusty, the old hound, drove the dog pound wagon right off the road. They had come to help Lady's friend.

Jim Dear and Lady soon arrived on the scene of the accident. Lady jumped out of the taxi and was very relieved to see that Tramp was safe. But, when she saw Trusty stuck under the carriage's wheel, her heart sank. Jock sat beside him howling.

"Darling, we should thank Lady's friends. Jock and Trusty risked their lives to keep Tramp from going to the pound," said Jim Dear. "We'll take Trusty to a veterinarian right away."

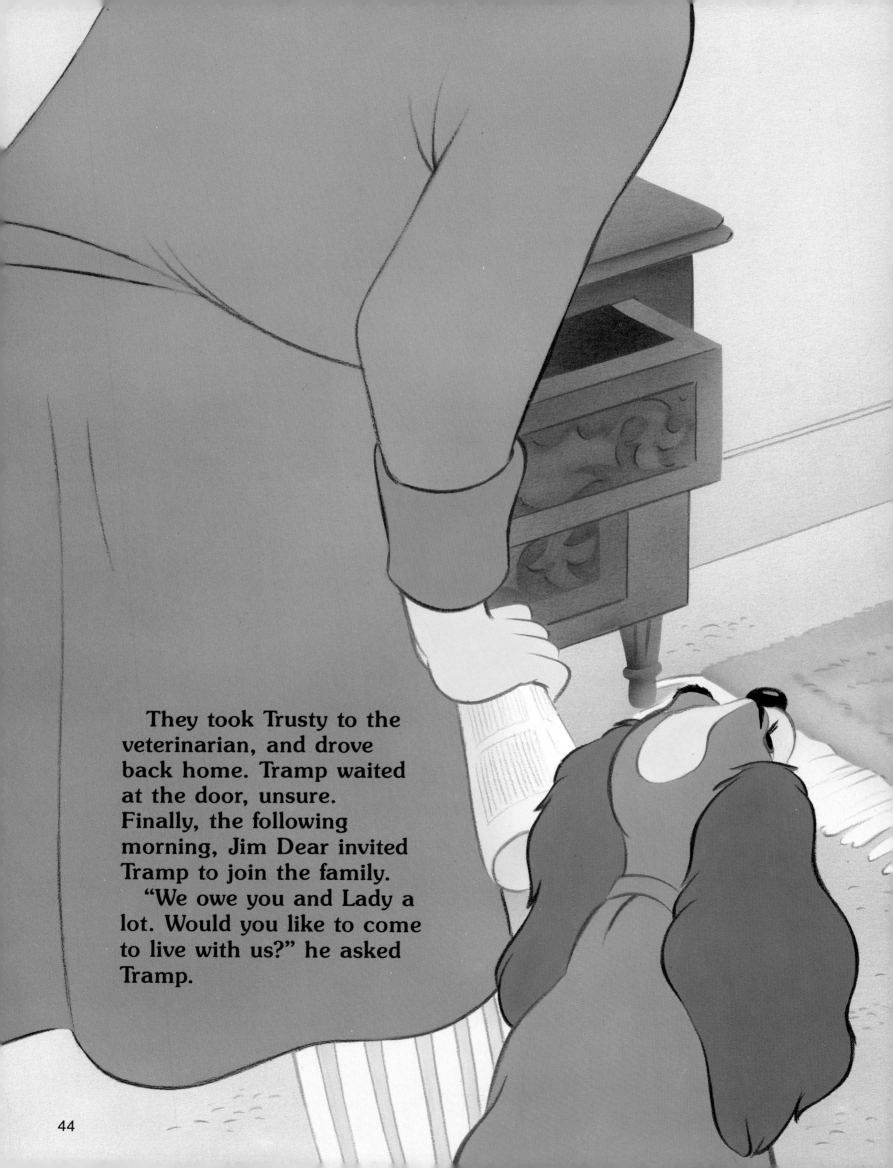

They took Trusty to the veterinarian, and drove back home. Tramp waited at the door, unsure. Finally, the following morning, Jim Dear invited Tramp to join the family.

"We owe you and Lady a lot. Would you like to come to live with us?" he asked Tramp.

"Me? Live in a house?" thought Tramp. "Well...if it's with Lady, sure!"

Jim Dear gave Tramp a beautiful collar with his name engraved on it.

It was Christmas again. Jock and
Trusty paid a visit to Lady and Tramp.

Tramp and Lady invited them to spend Christmas at Jim Dear and Darling's home. There were four new additions to the family that Christmas. Lady had given birth to four puppies—three girls and a boy.

"The girls look just like you, Lady!" said Jock.

"And the boy looks like you, Tramp!" added Trusty. "What a handsome family you are! This is the best Christmas I have had in years."

Tramp and Lady felt the same way. Life was just wonderful after all.

This 1988 edition published by Derrydale Books, distributed by Crown Publishers, Inc., 225 Park Avenue South New York, New York 10003

Produced by Twin Books 15 Sherwood Place Greenwich, CT 06830

Directed by HELENA Productions Ltd

Image adaption by Van Gool-Lefevre-Loiseaux

Printed and bound in Hong Kong

ISBN 0-517-66194-2

hgfedcba

The
Wonderful
World
of
Disney